THE CONJUROR'S COOKBOOK
GOBLIN STEW

D1332446

You can find out more about
Jonathan Emmett's books
by visiting his website at
http://www.scribblestreet.co.uk

THE CONJUROR'S COOKBOOK
GOBLIN STEW

JONATHAN EMMETT

ILLUSTRATED BY
COLIN PAINE

BLOOMSBURY
CHILDREN'S
BOOKS

For Rachel – J.E.
For Christine – C.P.

All rights reserved; no part of this publication may be
reproduced or transmitted by any means, electronic, mechanical,
photocopying or otherwise, without the prior permission
of the publisher

First published in Great Britain in 2000
Bloomsbury Publishing Plc, 38 Soho Square, London, W1V 5DF

Copyright © Text Jonathan Emmett 2000
Copyright © Illustrations Colin Paine 2000

The moral right of the author has been asserted
A CIP catalogue record of this book is available from the
British Library

ISBN 0 7475 4403 4

Printed in England by Clays Ltd, St Ives plc

10 9 8 7 6 5 4 3 2 1

Jake's granny was the most extraordinary cook. She could cook anything and everything. So, when Great Aunt Elinor sent her a strange book full of magical recipes, she didn't think twice about trying them out.

It was just as well that Jake was there to help out – you never know what might happen when you open The Conjuror's Cookbook.

A Mysterious Package

Jake's granny was the most extraordinary cook. She could cook anything and everything. She had written several best-selling cookbooks such as *Granny's Gorgeous Grub* and *Granny's Perfect Puddings*, but her great hobby was re-discovering strange and long-forgotten recipes such as:

Jam and Haddock Hotpot,
Roast Banana in Curry Sauce,
Stir-fried Spaghetti Soufflé
and *Beef and Onion Ice-cream*.

Some people said that these recipes should be left *long forgotten* because they sounded so revolting, but when Granny cooked them, they tasted delicious.

Jake's dad often said that 'Granny could cook a pair of old boots and make them tasty!' And Jake believed it. He thought that her cooking was wonderful and it made him want to be a cook himself one day.

So, Jake was delighted when Granny asked him if he'd like to spend a weekend at her cottage to do some cooking.

Granny's old cat, Delia, was dozing on the rug when a huge parcel spat through the letterbox and landed –SMACK– on top of her. She let out such a shriek that Jake and Granny rushed into the hall to see what had happened.

'There, there, dumpling,' said Granny, picking up the cat and giving her a squeeze.

Jake inspected the parcel. It looked very mysterious. The wrapping was dirty and battered and there was a strange foreign stamp on it. It looked as if it had travelled

half-way around the world.

'Go on,' said Granny, who could see how curious he was, 'open it.'

Jake tore away the paper to reveal a large book, with a letter tucked inside the cover.

'I bet it's from your Great Aunt Elinor,' said Granny, opening the letter.

Great Aunt Elinor was Granny's elder sister. She was an explorer and spent all her time travelling around the far-flung corners of the world.

'Fishsticks!' said Granny, rummaging in her apron. 'I haven't got my glasses. Could you read the letter for me, dear?'

Jake was happy to help. Great Aunt Elinor was always up to something exciting, so he wanted to know what was in the letter just as much as Granny did.

Here is what he read:

Dear Sister,

Sorry I haven't written for so long, but I've been off on one of my expeditions!

I've been looking for the Lost Palace of Sultan Peppa. The Sultan was known as 'The Conjuror' because he was supposed to be a great magician, able to conjure-up all sorts of weird and wonderful creatures. An old legend says that he conjured up a gang of giants and had them build a magnificent palace in the heart of the jungle. The local people believe that the Palace is still there and that The Conjuror still lives in it. So I thought I'd try and find it!

Off I went, squelching through swamps, wading across rivers and sharing my tiny tent with all sorts of creepy crawlies.

I had almost reached the end of my journey, when an extraordinary thing happened. I was deep in the jungle, hundreds of miles from anywhere, when I was woken up, in the middle of the night, by an almighty bang! The earth shook, wind blasted

11

the trees and the air was filled with smoke and steam and all sorts of strange smells.

I set off again the next morning, but instead of finding The Conjuror's Palace, I found a ruddy great hole the size of a football pitch!

And sitting in the middle of it, huddled over an empty cooking pot, was a ragged, wrinkly old man.

I think the old fellow had gone a bit bonkers because he told me that he was The Conjuror. He said that his palace had just exploded and that the hole was all that was left of it.

I didn't believe him of course, but I did ask him if he could conjure-up something - just to be sure. This made him rather angry. He said that he couldn't conjure-up anything because the goblins had thrown all of his magic ingredients into the pot. And that was why the palace had exploded in the first place.

Then I saw that he was sitting on this big book. The old man told me that it was his cookbook, but it was no use to him without his ingredients and that he'd gone right off home cooking anyway.

Well, I remembered how much you love nosing through strange recipes, so I gave him two cheese sandwiches and a packet of crisps and he let me have the book in return. I hope you like it!

I don't expect I'll be home for a while, but I will try to write again soon. Give my love to all the family - especially little Jake.

Best wishes,

Your loving sister

Elinor

Wriggling Words

'A conjuror's cookbook,' laughed Granny, clapping her hands. 'How extraordinary.'

Jake looked closely at the book. It was bound in some sort of skin that felt soft and strangely warm to the touch – almost as if it was alive!

He opened it and found that the pages were crammed with handwritten recipes.

At first Jake thought that they were written in a foreign language, but then the words seemed to wriggle about and, all of a sudden, he found that he could understand them.

'Did you see that?' exclaimed Jake, turning to Granny.

'See what?' asked Granny, who had been to fetch her glasses.

'The book!' said Jake. 'There's something funny about these recipes. I think I saw them moving.'

Granny took the book to the kitchen table and slowly turned the pages.

'Well, they don't seem to be moving now,' she said, 'but there's certainly something funny about them. They're the strangest recipes that I've ever come across.'

They flicked through the book, pointing things out and reading them aloud.

Most of the recipes had fantastic names like *Trolls on Toast*, *Serpent Soup* or *Dragon Dumplings*.

'That's funny,' said Jake, reading through the ingredients. 'There doesn't seem to be any serpent in the *Serpent Soup* or any dragon in the *Dragon Dumplings*. Perhaps it's a vegetarian cookbook.'

'Or perhaps it's because serpents and dragons don't exist,' laughed Granny. 'Mind you, I'm not sure that half of these ingredients do. I've never heard of "witchroot" or "trollberries" and I wouldn't know where to start looking for them.

'In fact . . .' she said, turning over the last page '. . . I don't think we have *all* the ingredients for any of these recipes.'

'That's a shame,' sighed Jake. 'They sound so exciting.'

Then a strange thing happened. The pages began to turn by themselves, flicking backwards until they fell open in the middle of the book.

'You did see that – didn't you?' said Jake excitedly. He was beginning to have a strange feeling about the book. There was something magical about it. Perhaps the old man *had* been a conjuror after all.

'I expect it was just a draught,' said Granny uneasily. She was too old to start believing in magic. She tried to close the

cookbook but it wouldn't stay shut. It kept springing open on the same page.

'Perhaps this was The Conjuror's favourite recipe,' said Jake. 'That's why it keeps falling open there.'

'Hmmm,' said Granny uneasily. It didn't feel like the book was just *falling* open. It felt like it was *opening itself*. She read the recipe carefully.

'Wait a minute!' she exclaimed. 'I think we've got all the ingredients for this one!'

'What's it called?' asked Jake eagerly.

'*Goblin Stew*,' said Granny.

She handed the book to Jake and this is what he read.

Goblin Stew

If you've never experienced the incredible smell and flavour of Goblin cooking you should definitely give this dish a try. It's an excellent recipe for beginners – it almost cooks itself – but be prepared for lots of cleaning up!

INGREDIENTS
2 buckets of rainwater
1 lump of root ginger
1 large piece of red herring
2 handfuls of bogey beans
1 small mouldy potato

First, find the biggest pot that you've got and make sure that it is the VERY biggest, don't use anything smaller or it will all end in tears!

Pour the water into the pot and bring to the boil. This will take a while, so you'll have plenty of time to prepare the other ingredients.

Cut the ginger into seven pieces, roughly equal in size, and bury them outside under a mossy stone – if you don't have a mossy stone you could use an old house brick, providing it isn't too clean.

Feed the herring to your cat – if you don't have a cat then STEAL one!

As soon as the water comes to the boil, add the bogey beans, remembering to turn around quickly seven times before throwing them over your shoulder.

Throw away the mouldy potato – it's of no use to anyone.

Leave to simmer for EXACTLY one hour before serving – and don't dare touch it in the meantime, NO MATTER WHAT HAPPENS!

'What a peculiar recipe,' said Jake. 'Bogey beans seem to be the only real ingredient. What are they?'

Granny was rummaging around in the larder. She came out clutching a dusty yellow jar.

'Here we are!' she said triumphantly. 'Your Great Aunt sent them to me three Christmases ago. They look a bit funny. I've never been quite sure what to do with them.'

She unscrewed the jar and shook some of the dried beans out onto her hand. They were yellow and wrinkly and they looked like – well they looked like they had been pulled out of somebody's nose.

'Yeuch!' said Jake.

'I know what you mean,' said Granny. 'But things often taste nicer than they look, especially when they're cooked properly. Let's give it a try.'

*

Jake fetched two buckets of rainwater from the water butt in the garden while Granny gathered the rest of the ingredients. She couldn't find a mouldy potato at first, but then she remembered throwing one away, a few days before, so she went and fished it out of the dustbin.

'It seems a bit silly taking it out, just to throw it away again,' she admitted, 'but

when I'm cooking something for the first time, I always keep strictly to the recipe.'

Jake dragged a huge cooking pot out of a cupboard and heaved it up onto the hob. The pot was so big that Jake could have sat inside it.

'Are you sure that this is the VERY biggest?' asked Jake, remembering the recipe.

'Positive!' said Granny, pouring in the rainwater and lighting the hob.

Then she took the ginger and cut it into seven pieces. They were all about the same size except one, which was quite a bit smaller.

'That'll have to do,' she said, handing them to Jake. 'There's a nice big mossy stone beside the water butt. Go and bury them under that.'

Next, Granny took the herring, sniffed it to see that it was still fresh and gave it to Delia, who couldn't believe her luck.

'Don't expect it every day,' warned

Granny, as the cat chewed the fish contentedly.

Jake came back in just as the water was coming to the boil.

'Time to add the beans,' he said.

Granny took two handfuls of the revolting yellow beans, spun around seven times and tossed them over her shoulder, into the boiling water.

'Heavens! That's made me quite dizzy!' she said, steadying herself on the table.

'One last thing!' said Jake, picking up the mouldy potato and dropping it back into the bin.

'Here we go!' said Granny, putting the pot to simmer and setting the timer for exactly one hour.

Surprising Smells

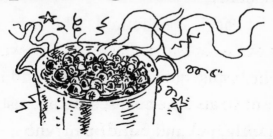

Jake stood on a chair and peeked into the pot.

'It's all right. I'm just looking,' he said. He hadn't forgotten that they were not to touch the pot now, *NO MATTER WHAT HAPPENED!*

'Come and see!' he said.

The beans were bobbing up and down excitedly on the surface of the water. Their yellow skins had turned bright red and they had swollen to the size of plums.

As Jake and Granny watched, the beans kept changing colour and swelling at an astonishing rate. A few seconds later and they looked like blue grapefruit.

Granny suddenly realised what would happen.

'Get back!' she shouted. 'They're going to pop!'

The beans, now bright purple and the size of footballs, squeezed up against the hot metal pot and burst open with a deafening bang!

Jake and Granny were blown clean off their feet and onto the kitchen floor.

They lay there for several minutes, shocked and breathless.

*

'Oh my giddy aunt!' said Granny at last.

'WOW!' gasped Jake.

But it was not the noise that had stunned them. It was the new SMELL that had accompanied it. The smell was neither pleasant nor unpleasant; it was just ABSOLUTELY UNBELIEVABLE!

'It's stupendous!' whispered Jake, frantically twitching his nose.

Granny took a long sniff and breathed slowly out.

'It's incredible,' she said distantly.

You see there are only so many smells in the world, just as there are only so many colours. If you were to come across a brand new colour, quite unlike anything anyone had ever seen, you would be so amazed that you wouldn't be able to take your eyes off it. So it was for Jake and Granny. They had just discovered a brand new smell and they couldn't take their *nostrils* off it! They forgot about everything and just lay there, sniffing and snuffling and trying to believe their noses.

Meanwhile, the new smell was wafting out of the kitchen window, across the countryside and into the nearby town of Egganham, where it astonished everyone that came across it . . .

Babies stopped crying,
cars drove into ditches,
builders fell off scaffolds,
postmen cycled into lampposts
and even the birds stopped singing!

Everyone and everything forgot what they were doing and fell silent when the smell reached them.

A group of bank robbers were so astounded that they walked out of the bank they'd just robbed, straight into a bed of quick-drying concrete. By the time they realised where they were, they were stuck solid! When the police found them, they had to carry them off in one big lump.

Antonio Morelli, Egganham's most expensive hairdresser, was just putting the finishing touches to Lady Toffingham's ringlets when the smell wafted into his salon. He was so surprised that he forgot what he was doing and cut off all of Lady Toffingham's hair. And Lady Toffingham was so distracted that she didn't even notice.

The smell went everywhere. It climbed up chimneys and dropped down drainpipes. It squeezed between the cracks in the pavement and squirmed around the backs of sofas. It crept up over sunlit rooftops. And it crawled down into the damp, dark earth beneath the mossy stone in Granny's garden.

Granny was the first to come to her senses. She climbed shakily to her feet.

'It's not over yet!' she said, checking the timer. 'There's still another three quarters of an hour before it's finished cooking.'

They peeped cautiously over the brim of the pot and were disappointed to find only a few centimetres of water, bubbling away at the bottom.

'We could turn down the heat and top it up a bit,' suggested Jake.

'I'm not sure,' said Granny doubtfully. 'We're not supposed to touch it at all.'

The astonishing smell had almost disappeared, but a cloud of steam now hung about the kitchen. Jake opened the back door, to clear the air, and was startled to find a little man standing on the doorstep.

Unexpected Guests

There was something very queer about
the visitor. His head, hands and feet were
far too big for the rest of his body. A
shock of ginger hair spilled out of a
grubby chef's hat onto an unusually wide
yellow face.

'You're A GOBLIN!' gasped Jake.

'And you is *A-GAPING*,' snapped the
little man. 'What of it?'

Granny started pinching herself. She
couldn't believe what she was seeing.

'What – what – what do you want?' she
stammered.

'Oh that's very nice, that is,' huffed the
goblin. 'Very polite! No "Hello's" or
"How-dee-doo-dee's", just a pair of

droopy-drop-jaws and "What does you want"!'

'You'll have to excuse us,' said Jake, remembering his manners. 'It's just that we're not used to receiving goblins. I'm Jake and this is Granny.'

'I is pleased to be meeting you,' said the goblin, taking off his hat and sweeping a low bow. 'Frogbottle, Master Chef at your service. My nosebuds couldn't help but be noticing that you is making Goblin Stew, which happens to be my speciality. Do you mind if I be coming in?'

The goblin didn't wait for an answer. By the time he had finished speaking he had skipped across the kitchen and up onto the hob.

'Spoon!' he demanded, peering into the pot.

Granny wasn't sure that she wanted the goblin anywhere near her cooking. His hands didn't look very clean and the smock he was wearing was covered in smears and stains.

'The recipe says that you're not supposed to touch it for another three quarters of an hour,' she told him.

'Wrong!' snapped Frogbottle. 'It says YOU is not supposed to be touching it! And *you* is *pea-poles*. It doesn't say nothing about *goblins*. Now, be bringing me a spoon.'

Granny handed the goblin a spoon and

he scooped out a mouthful of liquid.

'Not bad,' he said, smacking his lips.
'But it be needing more salt.'

Jake passed the salt-cellar and Frogbottle
unscrewed the top and emptied it all into
the pan.

'Better,' he said, taking another big sip.
'But it still be needing flour.'

'Now wait a minute,' said Granny. 'The recipe doesn't say anything about putting flour in!'

'Ah,' said Frogbottle, 'but the recipe doesn't say nothing about NOT to be putting *flour* in – does it?'

'That's not how recipes work!' said Granny hotly.

'How-things-is-working and how-things-is-being is two different plates of potatoes,' said Frogbottle.

'Besides,' he added, drawing himself up to his full height, which, even while standing on the hob, was still a few centimetres shorter than Granny, 'recipes is for beginners and I is a Master Chef. So you just be waddling off and fetching me the flour.'

Granny glared at the goblin. She didn't like being ordered about in her own kitchen, especially by someone so ill mannered.

'A *little bit* of flour can't hurt – can it?'

pleaded Jake. 'And Mr Frogbottle does
seem to know what he's doing.'

'Oh, all right then!' muttered Granny, 'but
don't blame me if it ends up as stodge!'

And she stomped off into the larder.

Frogbottle had decided to do without the
spoon and was now leaning into the pot
and taking a mouthful straight from the
bottom.

He didn't seem to mind that the liquid

was scalding hot or that flames were licking about his feet.

'How can you stand the heat?' asked Jake.

'I is used to it,' said Frogbottle. 'Hobs is my natural habitat. I is not just an ordinary goblin. I is a *hobgoblin*!'

Granny came back with a bag of flour and Frogbottle tore it open and dumped the whole lot into the stew.

'It's getting there,' he said, taking another mouthful. 'Do you be having any onions?'

Before Granny could answer, there was another knock at the door. Jake opened it and found a second ginger-haired goblin standing on the doorstep.

'Allow me to be introducing myself,' said the second goblin, who was also dressed as a chef. 'My name is Shrewbasher. I is something of an expert in Goblin Stew and I couldn't help but be noticing that —'

The goblin broke off as he caught sight of Frogbottle.

'WHAT'S HE DOING HERE?' he demanded, bounding up onto the hob.

'I got here first!' said Frogbottle fiercely.

'More's the pity!' said Shrewbasher, plunging his head into the pot and taking a mouthful of stew.

'Just as I thought!' he exclaimed, spitting the stew onto the floor. 'Too salty!'

'Codswhiffle!' shouted Frogbottle. 'It just be needing a few onions.'

'It'll be taking more than a few onions to be fixing this,' scoffed Shrewbasher, jumping down and scuttling into the larder.

'There's nothing to be fixing!' insisted Frogbottle, running after him.

Granny was about to follow them when there was more hammering at the door.

Too Many Cooks

Granny opened the door and four more ginger-haired goblins spilled into the kitchen and swarmed up onto the hob.

They didn't stop to introduce themselves, but their names were Snailsucker, Ratmasher, Crabfondle and Hogwasher.

Granny had almost closed the door again when another goblin squeezed breathlessly through the gap. He was quite a bit smaller than the rest and his name was Gnatsqueezer.

Frogbottle and Shrewbasher came out of the larder, with their arms piled high with food. They were outraged when they discovered the newcomers.

'I is in charge!' they both shouted, as they barged their way back to the pot.

But the other goblins had their own ideas and began to snatch away the ingredients.

There were now seven goblins in all.

'Let's hope that's the last of them,' said Jake.

'I'm not letting any more in!' said Granny, who was almost in tears. She felt like a stranger in her own kitchen.

The goblin's squabbling became louder and louder as they argued over whether or not the new ingredients should go into the stew. But, one by one, bit by bit, everything was dropped, thrown or spat into the pot.

When the last scrap of food had gone in, each goblin took a great gulp of stew before screaming his opinion.

'It be needing GARLIC!' bellowed Frogbottle.

'It be needing GOOSEBERRIES!'
shrieked Shrewbasher.

'It be needing HORSERADISH!' snarled
Snailsucker.

'It be needing HAMBURGERS!' roared
Ratmasher.

'It be needing APPLES!' cried
Crabfondle.

'It be needing ANCHOVIES!' howled
Hogwasher.

'It be needing cheese and onion flavoured CRISPS!' squealed Gnatsqueezer.

The goblins didn't bother to ask for any of these things, they just helped themselves. There was soon a frenzied traffic between pot and larder as the little chefs competed to add their chosen ingredients.

And the more food they added, the more frantic they became. They pulled apart packets, broke open bottles and tore into

tins, scraping out every last morsel and throwing it into the pot.

But for each mouthful that was put into the stew, the goblins took out another to taste. And so the pot was never filled.

Gnatsqueezer, the smallest goblin kept falling into the stew, where he would swim about coughing and spluttering until the other goblins hauled him out and tossed him aside.

After each such occasion, the wretched creature would pick himself up, glare meaningfully at Granny and say, 'It's just because I is smaller than them. It's all your fault!'

'What does he mean by that?' asked Jake.

'I haven't the foggiest,' said Granny.

The kitchen was beginning to look like a rubbish tip. Broken glass, empty tins and torn boxes lay everywhere. But the goblins were now squabbling so violently that Jake and Granny were too frightened to interfere.

'They can't keep adding food for ever,' said Jake hopefully. 'Sooner or later they'll run out.'

But as soon as they had finished stripping the larder, the goblins set about raiding the rest of the kitchen. First they ransacked the fridge and the freezer and then they started on the cupboards, punching and kicking each other to get at the contents.

They had worked themselves up into such a frenzy that Jake and Granny decided it would be safest to shelter beneath the kitchen table.

Jake looked on in amazement at the riot that was now raging around the stew pot.

'I can't believe that they still want to taste it,' he said. 'They must have swallowed five potfuls already. One of them will burst.'

'I don't think so,' said Granny glumly. 'None of the little rotters seem to be getting any fatter.'

There was a dreadful screech as

Ratmasher dragged Delia from her hiding
place behind the fridge.

'Cat!' he yelled excitedly. 'Just what I be
needing!'

'Oh no you don't!' said Granny fiercely.
She snatched Delia into her arms and gave
the goblin a threatening stare. 'Not my
little dumpling!'

Ratmasher spotted a stack of small tins beneath the sink.

'Cat food!' he said grudgingly. 'The next best thing!'

Soon there wasn't a scrap of food left in the kitchen, but the goblins kept on searching, as if looking for one last thing.

Frogbottle was scavenging through the rubbish on the table when he came across a dusty yellow jar.

'Here they is!' he cried triumphantly, as he scrambled back to the hob.

The other goblins stopped searching and raced after him. But by the time they reached him, Frogbottle had unscrewed the jar and emptied the entire contents into the stew.

'Are they what I think they are?' asked Granny, worried.

'I'm afraid so,' said Jake.

Loud squeaking and creaking noises came from the pot as an *entire jarful* of bogey beans began to swell rapidly inside it.

'Get away!' shouted Jake. 'It's going to explode!'

But the goblins didn't listen. Instead of abandoning the pot, they were fighting to get into it.

'It'll blow their heads off,' said Granny.

She didn't seem to be too upset by the idea.

'We'd better take cover!' said Jake.

They curled up beneath the table as . . .

KABOOOOM!

. . . an enormous explosion shook the cottage.

Dinner is Served

The sound of the explosion died away and Jake opened his eyes.

'Are you all right?' he asked.

'I think so,' said Granny dazedly. 'Although I can still hear a ringing in my ears.'

'I think that must be this,' said Jake. He rummaged around beneath a heap of cereal packets and pulled out the kitchen timer. The bell had just gone off. An hour had passed since Granny had set it.

'That means the stew's ready!' said Jake.

'What's left of it,' snorted Granny. 'Wait a minute! Where are the goblins?'

They crawled out from beneath the table and looked cautiously around them.

The goblins were nowhere to be seen.

Granny clambered over to the pot and
peeked into it.

It was all but empty.

'They've vanished!' gasped Jake.

'They could have offered to help tidy up
first!' said Granny, looking around the
remains of her kitchen. The floor was
covered with rubbish and there were splats
and spills everywhere.

'They didn't even say goodbye,' said
Jake.

'Well, I suppose I should just be thankful that they're gone!' sighed Granny.

Jake helped Granny clean up. They stuffed all the rubbish into plastic bags and then set to work scrubbing, washing and wiping the whole kitchen.

They found food and drink smeared over everything. They didn't finish until well after midnight.

The only thing that had stayed clean was the cookbook. It was lying open where they'd left it, without so much as a crumb on it.

Granny shut the book and this time it stayed shut.

'Well there's no doubt that this belonged to a real conjuror,' she said, pushing the book onto a high shelf. 'But as for cooking the recipes – NEVER AGAIN!'

'But it was kind of fun,' said Jake wistfully.

'Watching my kitchen get ransacked by a

gang of greedy goblins is not what I call fun,' said Granny sharply. 'And having no food left for supper isn't either.'

'You're right about that,' groaned Jake. 'I'm starving!'

'Me too,' said Granny. 'But it's too late to go out for food now.'

They had hoped to discover some food that the goblins had overlooked but they hadn't found so much as a cornflake.

'There's a few drops of stew left in the pot,' said Jake doubtfully. 'Do you think we should try it?'

'We might as well,' said Granny. 'It's the only thing left!'

Granny held the heavy pot upside down while Jake scraped the few remaining drops into a dish.

The stew looked grey and unappetising and there was only enough for two spoonfuls, one for each of them.

'Here goes!' said Jake, as they popped the spoons into their mouths.

'It's not bad,' said Granny surprised. 'In fact . . . it's rather . . . delicious!'

'It tastes like thick creamy tomato soup,' agreed Jake smacking his lips, 'with freshly baked bread.'

'And crispy deep-fried mushrooms,' added Granny.

'And ripe juicy melon,' said Jake excitedly.

'And smoked mackerel pâté,' said Granny, her eyes widening.

And it didn't stop there as one after another, a thousand glorious flavours filled their mouths. They felt as if they were eating an enormous banquet instead of a single spoonful.

The soups and starters gave way to a mouth-watering selection of main courses – fine fillets of fish in rich creamy sauces, tender savoury meats with crisp roast potatoes, roast fowl with succulent vegetables and hot spicy curries with cool fresh salads.

Then came the desserts – pastries as light as a breath, ice-creams as soft as a whisper, cakes as fluffy as clouds and puddings so sweet they could break your heart.

The stew tasted of every delicious food that you could imagine, all the things that the goblins had put into it, and many they had not. It was so wonderfully yummy that Jake and Granny could not bring themselves to swallow a single drop. They just rolled it about on their tongues and let it trickle down slowly into their stomach, until it had all disappeared.

'That was superb!' sighed Granny afterwards, sinking back into her chair. 'Quite the best meal I've ever had.'

Jake sat rubbing his tummy. 'I feel like I've eaten enough to last me for a month!' he said dreamily.

A Second Helping?

Jake could still taste the wonderful stew days after he'd finished it and it was weeks before he wanted, or needed, to eat anything else.

He looked healthy enough and he wasn't getting thin, but Jake's mum and dad were still very worried about him. They cooked all his favourite foods, spaghetti bolognese and sticky toffee pudding, but he just wasn't interested.

'I'm sure it's very nice,' he said politely, after turning down a mouth-watering triple fudge sundae. 'But it won't be as good as Granny's Stew.'

'Perhaps we should get her to cook some more of that?' suggested Jake's mum, who was desperate to see him eat something.

'I don't think that she'd want to,' said Jake doubtfully.

Jake hadn't told his mum and dad about the goblins. He and Granny had decided to keep it a secret, since no one would believe them anyway.

'Nonsense,' said Dad. 'There's nothing your granny likes doing better than cooking.'

But Granny couldn't cook any more of the stew, even if she had wanted to. The goblins had used up all of the bogey beans.

'Don't worry about Jake not wanting to eat,' she told his parents. 'I was the same myself. It'll wear off in a couple more days and he'll be as hungry as ever.

And to Mum and Dad's relief, she was right.

It was a long time before Granny managed to get her kitchen restocked with food and ingredients. When Jake went to visit her a few weeks later, she said that she still hadn't finished.

'I've got all the ordinary things,' she admitted, 'but there are still a few *special* things that I want. I've asked your Great Aunt Elinor to try and get them for me.'

A smile spread slowly across Jake's face.

'What kind of special things?' he asked.

'Oh you know,' said Granny winking, '*witchroot, trollberries*, that sort of thing.'

'But I thought you said "never again",'
said Jake.

'Well, I'm not sure about Goblin Stew,'
said Granny slowly. 'I don't think I could
bear to go through all that again, but
perhaps I –'

'Perhaps *we*,' interrupted Jake hopefully.

'Well,' said Granny grinning, 'perhaps *we*
might try one of the other recipes . . .'

Goblin Stew

If you're lucky enough to have a jar of bogey beans, you could try cooking Goblin Stew for yourself. They must be real bogey beans though – picked at the stroke of midnight from a bogey beanstalk and left to dry on the rim of a volcano – and not just something you pulled out of your nose!

If you can't get hold of any bogey beans, you might like to try this recipe instead. **But make sure you get a grown-up to help you!** It's not as mouth-bogglingly wonderful as the real Goblin Stew, but it is very tasty and it does smell *surprisingly* good! And there's a lot less tidying up to do afterwards!

INGREDIENTS
(For 3-4 people)
450 g (1 lb) Diced Lamb
700 g (1 ½ lb) Onions
450 g (1 lb) Carrots
3 Tablespoons of Flour
600 ml (1 pint) Water
3 Tablespoons of Vegetable Oil
1 Stock Cube
Salt and Pepper
1 Small Mouldy Potato

This stew is very easy to prepare but it does need to be left to cook for a long time. So you should start preparing it about 2½ hours before you want to eat.

The first thing you need to do is chop up the meat and vegetables – but be careful! When a goblin chops a finger off he can just throw it into the stew and grow another, but if you chop off one of yours, you've lost it for good. So you might want to get your grown-up to do this bit for you! The onions and the carrots need to be peeled and cut into slices about 1 cm thick and the lamb needs to be chopped into 3 cm cubes.

Put the flour into a flat dish or tray and add a

couple of pinches of salt and pepper. Place the meat in the dish and keep turning it over until it's covered in flour.

Put the water into a jug or bowl and crumble the stock cube into it.

Next, get a large saucepan with a lid – it doesn't have to be big enough to sit inside, just big enough to put your head in. Heat the oil in the saucepan, put in the onions and fry them on a medium heat for 4 minutes, turning them over all the time.

Add the meat to the saucepan and fry for another 5 minutes and keep turning it over! Turn up the heat and add the water slowly, stirring the stew until it comes to the boil.

Add the carrots and a couple more pinches of salt and pepper and then turn the heat down until the stew is ONLY JUST BUBBLING! If there is too much heat, the stew will bubble up out of the saucepan and escape! So make sure you get it just right.

Put the lid on the saucepan and leave to bubble gently for 2 hours. But take a look at it every half-hour or so to check that it's not escaping!

Serve up with bread and butter and enjoy!

Oh . . . and throw away the mouldy potato – it's of no use to anyone.

Vegetarian Alternative:

If you don't want to use meat, you can use a myco-protein such as Quorn instead. In which case, you should add the flour straight to the pan, mixing it in thoroughly, before adding the water. You need about 300g (11oz) of myco-protein and you can cut the cooking time to 1 hour.